For NATE HOWARD,
who tamed the savage kitty

TS	THIS BOOK HAS BEEN RATED **T E R R I B L Y S I L L Y** Some material may be too silly for grown-ups.

All the animals used in these photographs are the author's pets.
No harm came to them in the making of this book.

One dark and perilous night, three mouse explorers
sailed toward a strange, uncharted island.

Captain Charles Limburger steered the tiny vessel,
while Doctor Vincent Varmint and his beautiful assistant,
Rosie Rodent, looked on.

When they reached the island, the three explorers were astonished. A group of natives was performing an ancient ceremony, offering up a sacrificial can of tuna fish and repeating a mysterious chant:

"Heeeer, Ki-tee Ki-tee!

Heeeer, Ki-tee Ki-tee!

Heeeer, Ki-tee Ki-tee Ki-tee!"

Suddenly, the island began to tremble.

Crashing through the thick forest came the most frightening creature ever known to mousekind: the mighty Kat Kong!

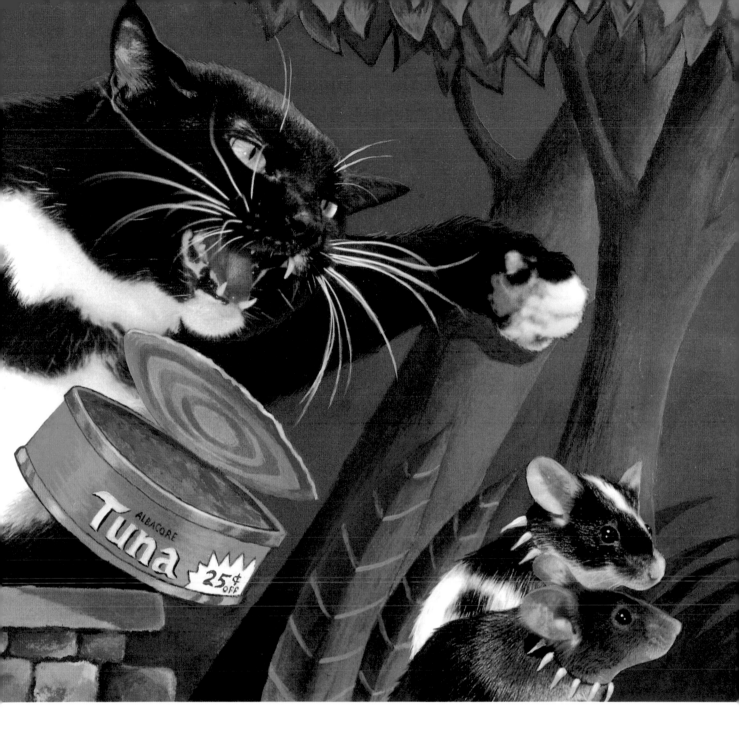

Meowing and hissing ferociously, the colossal cat took three giant kitty steps . . .

. . . and tripped over the tuna fish can. Klunk!
Kat Kong bumped his head on the ground and was
knocked out cold.

"If only we could bring him back to the city with us," said Doctor Varmint.

"No," replied Rosie Rodent, "it would be wrong to take this creature away from its natural habitat just to satisfy our scientific curiosity."

"Forget science," squeaked Doctor Varmint. "Think of the money we could make!"

So the three explorers wrapped Kat Kong in a giant burlap bag and tied him tightly to the ship.

As they sailed back to the great city of Mousopolis, they took special care not to let the cat out of the bag.

Several days later in downtown Mousopolis, Doctor
Varmint unveiled his discovery to a sold-out crowd.

"Ladies and gentlemice," he squeaked. "I give you
Kat Kong: the nine-lived wonder of the world!"

The audience cheered.

Kat Kong, however, was not amused. The towering tomcat hissed and meowed wildly.

"Do not be afraid," Doctor Varmint told the crowd.

"There is no way this creature can escape!"

"I repeat—there is NO WAY this creature can escape!…

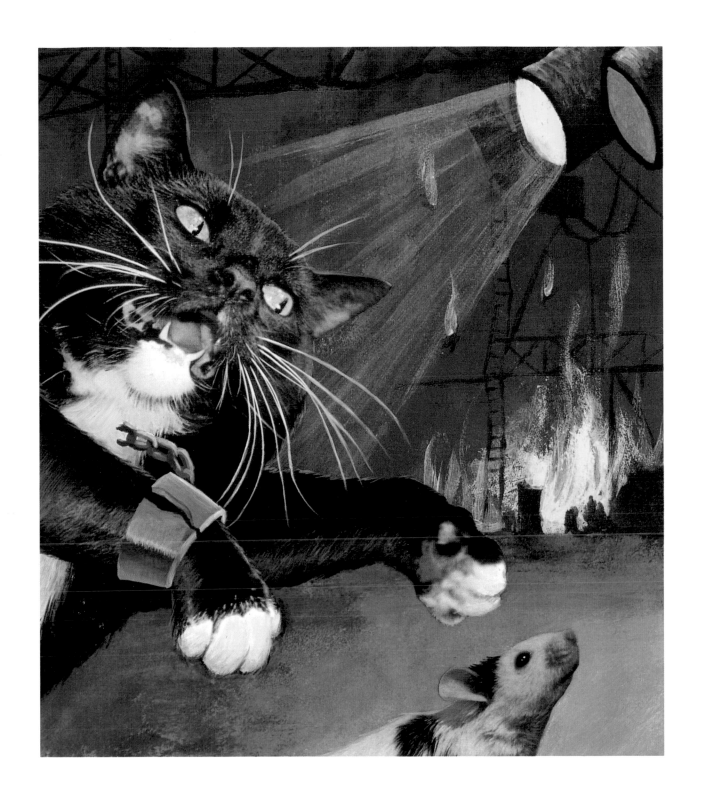

Well, aah—actually, I *could* be wrong about that."

Soon the city of Mousopolis was in a panic. The
ferocious feline tore through the streets, knocking down
buildings, ripping out power lines, and generally causing
quite a ruckus!

Captain Charles Limburger rushed off to organize a counterattack team, while the beautiful Rosie Rodent watched the destruction from her apartment window. "Help!" cried the engineer. "The cat's got my train!"

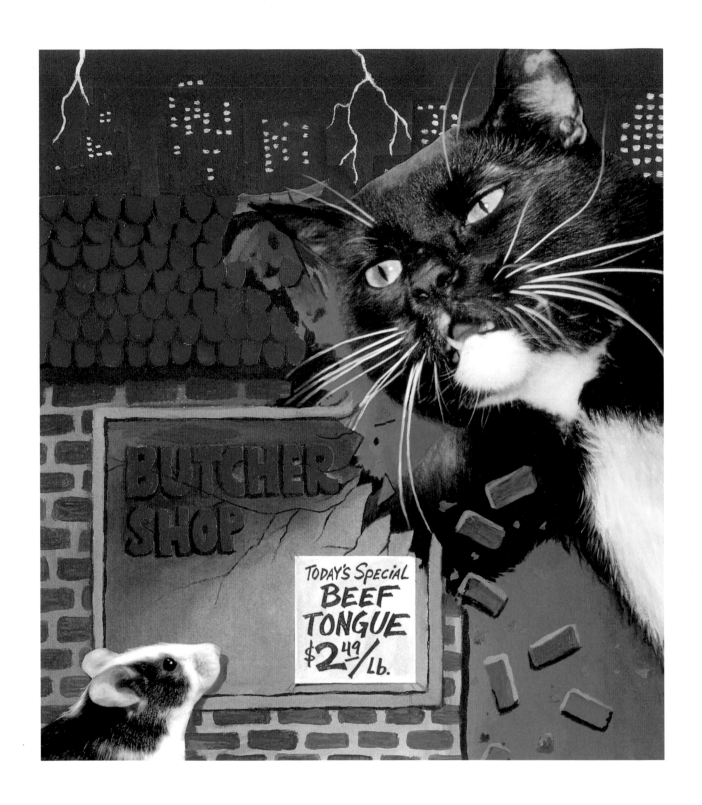

"Help!" squeaked the butcher. "The cat's got my tongue!"

"Help!" shrieked Rosie. "The cat's got me!"

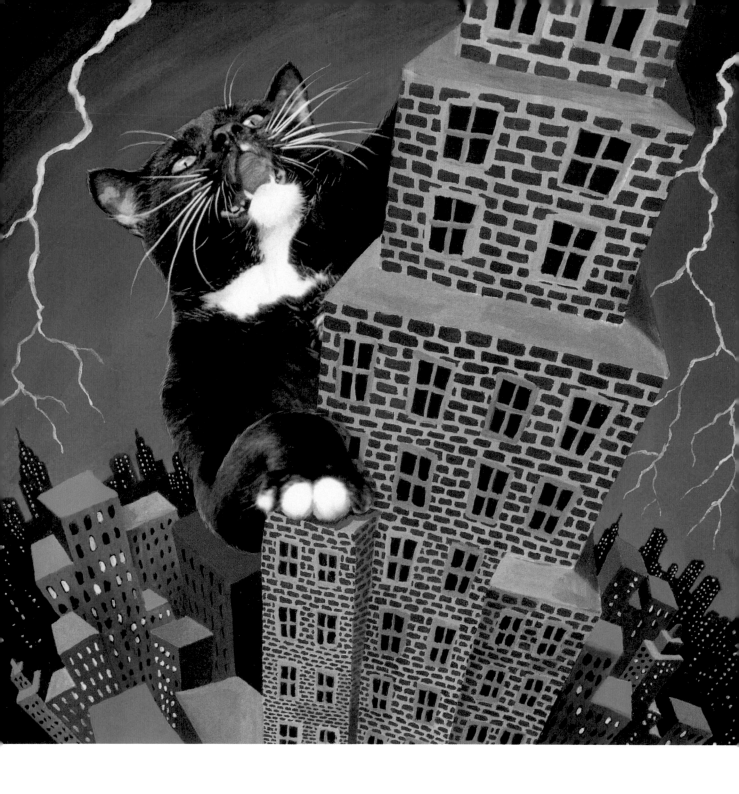

Soon the crazed cat was heading straight for the top
of the Romano Inn . . .

. . . with the beautiful Rosie tailing behind.

A fleet of airplanes quickly flew into action, but their weapons were useless against the meowing menace. It seemed as if *nothing* could stop the terrifying Kat Kong.

Then, suddenly, a squeaking ray of hope rocketed through the thick clouds of gloom and despair. Captain Charles Limburger to the rescue!

Captain Limburger had a plan. He swooped close to Kat
Kong and held out a red package tied with gold ribbons.

"Hey, Kat!" he shouted. "Look what I've got!"

He circled again and again shouting, "You'll never guess
what's inside this package!"

Kat Kong stared intensely at the red package. With each passing second, the colossal kitty's interest grew and grew. Finally, Kat Kong could stand it no longer—he *had* to find out what was inside that package! With one swift paw, the puzzled pussycat reached out for the red package, and lost his balance.

"MMMMMMMMMMMMMMMMMMMEEEEEEEEEEEEEEE

OOOOOOOOOOOOOOOwwwwwwwwwwwwwWWWWW!"

When the dust settled, a crowd of mice gathered to
view the final resting place of the mighty Kat Kong.
"He's fallen," said one mouse.

"And he can't get up," said another.

"Well," said the chief of police, "it looks as if beauty killed the beast!"

"No," said Doctor Varmint as he looked sadly into the glowing red horizon. "It was curiosity. Curiosity killed the cat!"